SCREAM WITH ME

SCREAM WITH ME

Volume I

D.W. SAUR

Polar Press

Scream With Me: Volume I

By D.W. Saur

© Copyright 2023 D. W. Saur

Scream With Me Content Warning

The content discussed in this story you're about to read discusses potentially sensitive topics that include but are not limited to physical and substance abuse, addictions, paranormal and supernatural, extraterrestrial, mythological, and graphic violence that may be triggering to some. The goal of this work is to entertain and not cause harm. The author does not intend to undermine the struggles of people who have suffered or been victims. Please stop reading when any parts of the stories become too much.

In Memory of

Kevin and Chris

Unconditional Love: Part I

"So girls." I slapped my hands together, brushing off the salt left behind from the fries. "I know the past few years haven't been easy."

That's an understatement. Jonathan left for work three years ago and never came home. It's been two years since we lost the house and moved into the long-stay motel.

With a burger raised toward her lips, Ashley interjected, "Sounds like there's a but coming."

"But I have a surprise for you." I pulled my phone out of my jacket pocket and tapped on the newest picture. "What do you think?" In the photo, I was standing in front of a house holding a sold sign. They couldn't see the second floor or the poor state of the house from the picture, but I could see the excitement in the girls. Their eyes widened as they used to on Christmas morning. "I know it isn't much now, and there is a lot of work to do."

"But it's ours, right?" Brittany asked.

I fought away tears and nodded. They pushed back their chairs with such an eruption that they almost fell over. In a flurry, they ran to me, wrapping their arms around me.

"Thank you," Ashley said.

"Love you, Mom," Brittany added.

"Thank you, girls. I promise we'll get everything we lost back." I wiped the tears from my eyes. "Would y'all like to go see it?"

"Yes!" they both squealed.

We got into the car and headed for East End, named after the county's largest cemetery. It also just so happens to be neighboring my backyard. This and the state of the house is why I was able to get such a good deal on the home, but we needed out of the motel. It was a bit of a haul from the diner, so I pulled into the driveway twenty minutes later. With the car in park, I looked in the rearview mirror. The girls were just as wide-eyed as they were when they saw the picture.

"It's got a second floor. Do we get separate bedrooms?" Ashley's voice went up another octave. Her hands covered her face from embarrassment.

"Yes, you each get a room," I replied.

They jumped out of the car and I followed them to the door. The exterior didn't need as much work as the interior. The paint was chipping away and a fresh coat would be the cheapest way to bring it back to life. I put the key into the door and Brittany did the rest.

She turned the key, then the knob, and pushed the door open. They both rushed in and the state on the inside didn't bother them: the layers of dust, the discolored wood floor, the broken cabinet doors. The list goes on, but none of it bothered them. Ashley, almost sixteen now, rushed up the stairs. Brittany, almost twelve, was close to her sister's heels. They needed this small piece of happiness as much as I did. As they scurried about upstairs, I went back to the car.

I opened the trunk and pulled out three boxes containing air mattresses. Our old beds have been gone since before we lost the house. With my arms full, I closed the trunk and headed back inside. Ashley was on her way down the steps and jumped from the fourth step to the landing.

"Can we stay the night?" she asked.

From the top of the stairs, Brittany shouted, "Can we?"

"We've got to get a change of clothes but I got these for us until I can afford proper beds."

Ashley grabbed the boxes from my hands. "Can we camp out in the living room tonight?"

"Yeah, Mom, can we?" Brittany started coming down the stairs.

"Sure, but let's go get some of our things."

We didn't have much and could have crammed the car fully, but we had the motel room for a few more days so there was no need to rush. As we drove, the girls sang and danced in their seats. I jumped in with the songs I knew but I just wanted to soak it in. It's been a long time since I've seen them this happy and I took every chance I could to glance at them in the mirror.

I didn't even have the car in park when the girls jumped out and ran into the room. They were ready as soon as I entered, so I quickly grabbed some clothes and rushed back to the car. As we started back to our new home, I decided to make a quick detour and grab a pizza. I don't think anyone was hungry, but I thought it was something small that could make the night a bit more special.

"I'm stuffed." Ashley tossed the crust of her slice into the box.

"I'm tired and didn't even do anything today," Brittany added.

"How about we call it a night? I have tomorrow off and I want to get to cleaning first thing."

With a burst of energy, Brittany asked, "Can we help?"

"You have school tomorrow," I reminded.

"It's Friday, Mom." I just stared at Ashley. "It'll either be videos or games. I'm sure we won't miss anything."

"Fine, but there will be no sleeping in and no taking breaks. We have work to do. Agreed?"

"Agreed," they answered.

I got up, turned off the overhead light, and walked back to my bed. The girls quickly fell asleep, but nothing I did got me close to resting. I'd love to say it was the excitement of the house but it was something else, something more unsettling. The hours wore on but the feeling remained.

"Mom.... Mom."

"What?" I moaned. I didn't want to wake up. It felt like I'd just fallen asleep.

"Mom, wake up. I think someone's in the house."

I bolted up. My eyes were wide open but blurry. Even if my vision was clear, my head jerked around so quickly that I couldn't focus on anything. My heart was racing, beating so fast I swear it was going to burst through my chest. I was short of breath, like I was having a panic attack. Though the fright was real, all terror vanished as my vision cleared and I saw Ashley and Brittany.

They were safe and though Ashley was holding Brittany tight, there was something not right. It took me a moment to realize that the lights were shining brightly in every room except ours.

"Did you turn on the lights?" I asked.

"No. Brit woke me just a few moments ago when the kitchen light woke her."

"Then what?"

"The rest on the first floor turned on and then the lights turned on upstairs." Brittany pointed to the light shining down.

"Did you see anyone?"

"No," they answered.

"Okay. Stay here and I'll go check it out."

I slowly stood up. I tried to put on a brave face, but I could feel my knees shaking. My first step was no longer than a baby step and the creek of the floorboard made me wince. I took a deep breath and with clenched fists, I walked over and turned on the living room light so the girls wouldn't be in the dark. Of course, I didn't want to be in the dark, but I also didn't want to walk into a well-lit room not knowing who could be in there.

Each creek of the floor caused the pit in my stomach to grow larger. Besides lights being on that shouldn't, there was an eerie silence in the house. Yes, the floors are creaking, but that's all. I couldn't hear the air conditioning running, the refrigerator, or even nature's buzz outside. It was like we were trapped in a void. Making my way into the kitchen, my legs were still unsteady.

Why would someone come in and turn the lights on? There are far more vile things they could've done to three sleeping women. How could they go unseen by the girls?

I looked all about the first floor and saw no sign of anyone. I crept up the stairs and searched each room, including the closets. Aside from dust and grime, there was nothing there. I turned off the lights and headed back downstairs.

"Did you see anything?" Ashley asked.

"Nothing. I think it could be a wiring issue." I hoped. "I know a guy who can come take a look."

"Are you sure?" Brittany looked scared out of her mind and, to be honest, so was I.

"Yes." I looked at my phone. The alarm would be going off in less than half an hour. "I know you're not going to school this morning, but you would've been getting up soon anyway, so how about we go get breakfast?"

Driving to the diner, I kept asking myself question after question: *Was it really bad wiring? Could one of us have been sleepwalking? But Ashley saw it too, so it couldn't have been sleepwalking, right?* The only thing that made sense was the fear I felt. Goosebumps had prickled my arm and I couldn't shake the sinking feeling that something was wrong.

After a large breakfast, we cleaned out the motel and did the best we could to move on from the terror of last night. I think the girls shook it off quicker than I did. We went straight to work when we got to the house, but the thought of what caused the lights to turn on weighed heavily on my mind.

In almost a blink of an eye, a night's stay turned into a week, and a week turned into a month. An entire month passed with no incident, but the monthly anniversary of our first night in the house changed everything.

"Mom!"

Brittany's scream was bloodcurdling. I jumped from my bed

and ran into the hall. Ashley was already in Brit's room, holding her. Tears flowed down her cheeks. Her eyes were closed, and her entire body shaking.

"Brit, baby. What's wrong?" I kneeled at her bedside, placing my hand on her leg.

"There's something here."

I looked around. "Where? Show me."

"It went out of the room."

"What was it? Can you remember what it looked like?"

"There wasn't much to see. It was like a shadow, but it was tall and it wore a mask."

"What did the mask look like?"

"It had horns coming out the top, middle, and sides. He took it off and whispered—"

"What did he say?"

"I know."

"What? That's all? *He knows*? What does he know?"

"I don't know." She pointed to the door. "He walked out the door and the light turned on when he left. I couldn't move or say anything until he was gone."

I didn't even think about the lights. "Have you left upstairs?"

"No. I came straight to Brit's room once I heard the scream," Ashley answered. Brit shook her head no.

I got up and rushed to the stairs. The hallway and stairway lights were both on. I quickly made my way to the first floor. The living room lights were on. I turned to the kitchen and the same was true. I walked to the small dining room and the lights were on there also. Next, I checked the doors. The locks and the dead-bolts were secured. I checked all the windows and there wasn't a single sign anyone had gotten into the house or left. I rushed back upstairs to Brit's room.

"Did you see anything?" Ashley asked.

"Nothing. He's gone, but I'll go to the store and pick up some security cameras when it opens. Why don't y'all come to my room and we will try to rest before the alarm goes off?"

I led the way as they pulled their air mattresses behind them. I don't know if Brit was imagining what happened but I was so scared I locked the door behind them. For the moment there was no telling if she was just seeing things or telling the truth, but that simple act of securing the lock gave me a little more peace of mind.

I helped them get settled by my mattress and then I finally laid back down. However, I couldn't sleep. The look on Brit's face was haunting. And the way she was shaking? It wasn't just a nightmare. It was almost volatile. If she were dreaming, it had to feel like the most realistic dream one could have.

But what if she wasn't? What if what she saw was real? But it couldn't be. It took me no more than a minute to get to her room. How could someone leave the house that quickly and not make a sound? There were no footsteps or signs of anyone here. I reached for my phone and 5:45 a.m. shined brightly from the home screen. *When did Brit yell? It had to be around 5:30 a.m.. It was half an hour before the alarm went off.*

Thinking of the importance of the time kept me up, and as soon as the alarm blared, I jumped from my mattress. I brushed off my fright like I had a cramp, but I don't think the girls bought it, even in their barely-awake state.

Just like the last incident, I rushed them out the door after getting dressed. I dropped them off at school and then went to the store to purchase the security cameras. Paying hundreds of dollars for three cameras wasn't what I wanted to do, but I needed to see what was happening.

Luckily, the installation was simple. I just needed a power outlet, a few screws for the mount, an app, and a secure Wi-Fi connection. I placed one at the front door, one at the back, and one inside looking down the stairway. All were up and running in less than an hour.

What took place next became an obsession. I constantly looked at the app to see if anything was happening. Another month rolled by, and nothing. I never saw a light turn on, a shadow dance on the wall, or a person taking a stroll. There was nothing. Then...

"Mom...Please stop!"

"Mom... Mom! Mom, help!"

Brit and Ashley were both yelling for me. I dropped the ingredients for the dinner I was cooking and flew upstairs. I got to Brit's room first and she was on the ground crying while holding her back as best she could.

"What's wrong baby?"

"My back!"

I lifted her shirt. Red lines fissured up and down, side to side. They weren't cuts, and she wasn't bleeding, but it was clear that something attacked her.

"Oh my god, baby."

"Mom," Ashley sobbed.

I got up and ran next door. Ashley was on her knees with her face toward the floor. "Are you hurt?"

"It's my—"

"Your what?" she could only point to her butt. I walked over and crouched beside her on the floor. "I need to look." She shook her head. I pulled her shorts back slightly and each cheek was redder than Santa's suit. "What happened?"

Still sobbing, she answered, "I was just standing there, about to walk out, and then something hit me."

"Hit you how?"

"Like I was being punished. It hurt so much and happened so fast. It was one right after another."

"Was anyone up here?"

"No."

"Mom," Brit said.

"Yes, baby." I held out my arms for her to come to me.

"I don't want to live here anymore."

I took her in my arms and cried.

The next day, I called a realtor and started making plans to move. I was anxious to get home to let the girls know, but when I stepped inside the house my foot didn't hit just the solid floor. My shoe was immediately soaked. I looked around to find the surface flooded with water. It flowed down the stairs, dripping from the ledge, and pooling on the first floor. Thinking the worst, I rushed upstairs to the bathroom and opened the door, but no one was there. Just the tub overflowing. The handle was turned all the way and water gushed out.

I turned off the faucet and rushed from room to room. The girls were nowhere to be found. I called Ashley's cell phone. It started ringing, and I made out the drum tune coming from upstairs. Running into Ashley's room, I saw her phone sitting on her mattress. My heart was beating out of my chest in sync with the ringtone. At that moment, the beat of my heart stopped altogether and sank into the pit of my stomach. *Something is terribly wrong.* I hung up and called 911. I tried to explain all that happened but I don't think they believed me.

When the police officers arrived I walked them through everything, starting from the time I came home. They took notes and listened intently, and I mentioned all that had happened before today too. It felt as though this went from the girls being kidnapped to I'm the lead suspect.

"Well, you have cameras, so can we look at them?" Officer Stevens asked.

"Yes." I pulled out my phone, opened the app, and handed it over so they wouldn't think I was up to something.

Several minutes passed. "We see both kids entering but neither of them leaving. Is it possible that they snuck out a window?"

"No, there's no reason for them to leave me. I'm all they have left."

"If you can spare a couple of pictures and give us a list of places they would normally visit; we can patrol throughout the night. We'll issue an Amber alert."

I found a couple of pictures in my purse and wrote a few addresses down even though I knew they weren't there. "Here you go."

"We'll keep a lookout for them and keep you posted. If you hear anything, let us know."

They left and I was far from finding the girls. I didn't know where they were, but I knew that this visitor of ours was behind it. There was nothing I could do but wait. Instead of just sitting and crying, I grabbed the mop and bucket and started cleaning. With each stroke I dug hard into the wood, pushing more water away than soaking it up. I kept this up for no clue how long when suddenly my phone dinged. I looked at the notification just as someone knocked at the front door. I opened the app and looked at the camera.

"Girls!" They were just standing at the door. "Girls! Come in!" I dropped the mop and ran to the door. "Get in here!" I was so relieved. "You scared—"

The door was wide open but the girls weren't there. I looked back at my phone and they were there. They were standing right in front of me on the screen. I held my phone up high and watched as the girls came in and headed up the stairs toward my room. I cautiously and slowly followed. Everything fiber in me told me not to follow. This was not right but I had to go.

I turned the corner and entered my room. It was empty. My room wasn't on a security camera so I switched from the app to the camera on my phone. To the right of my mattress were the girls and behind them was *IT*, the one terrorizing us. He was tall, thin, and looked like a shadow. The head had horns just like Brit said and the fingers that rested on the girls were like daggers. I couldn't see eyes, mouth, or anything else discernible and I knew I didn't want to. The shadow was frightening enough.

"What do you want!" I screamed.

"I have what I want," he growled. His hands stroked their hair. They didn't speak but I could see the tears pouring. "I've come for their sin."

"What sin?" I yelled. "They're great kids!"

"Go on. Tell her," he urged.

"I'm sorry Mom," Ashley sobbed. "I couldn't take it anymore."

"Take what? What are you talking about?"

"Dad. He hurt us every chance he got and I couldn't take it anymore." she looked down. "He took us to the Ridge. You know at his favorite spot overlooking the lake where he drives up to the edge. He got his belt out and told me to bend over. I saw the tire iron and I was so tired of it. So, after his first hit, I grabbed the iron, turned, and swung. When he was on the ground I kept hitting until I couldn't."

I fell to the ground. The horror that my kids were being abused and I didn't know was too much. I cried uncontrollably.

"Ashley and I put him in the car. She put the car in drive and it went into the lake."

"For this, I have come."

"You can't. They did what they had to. You must understand that. You have to! He gave them no other choice. Please, let them go!"

"I come for the sin, not the cause. There is someone else who handles that." He looked down at the girls and my skin crawled. "But I don't like children as much—" He stopped and my hopes immediately lifted. "So, let's make a deal."

"Anything, just please let them go," I pleaded.

"A sin of yours for theirs." His voice was almost giddy.

"What?"

"I find your sin and you take their place."

I felt a lump in my throat. My heart fell to my stomach. There's so much I want to do but I can't let the girls suffer. I nodded.

"Mine for theirs." I looked at the girls. Their tears continued to flow but their voices remained silent. "I love you, girls."

I closed my eyes and waited for *IT* to find what it needed. At first, I thought nothing was going to happen, but suddenly I felt it—a cold that the living cannot experience.

I couldn't breathe. I couldn't speak. I was powerless.

The cold started to spread through me like the blood in my veins. It spread to my toes, my fingers, and even to the top of my head.

It was the touch of death.

"Ah, yes, there it is." He pulled away. "I will come at 5:30."

So now I wait. Why wait until 5:30? Why did he choose this time? I should have pieced it all together sooner but I failed my children once more. 5:30 was the last time I saw Jonathan. Every morning, like clockwork, he left the house at 5:30. Maybe I could've prevented all this and spared the girls from this experience.

As I waited, I wrote all this down as best as I could because I didn't know what would happen when the alarm went off. I wrote it all so the person who would be reading it would know I didn't harm the girls. I did what I could to save them. I did what any mother would've done, so please someone take care of my girls.

Ash and Brit: If you're reading this know that I'm so sorry for all your father put you through. I wish I had known but I refuse to fail you again. Please forgive me, but know I love you both.

I laid the pen gently on the table.

Moments later time was up. 5:30 struck the clock but no alarm went off.

The only sound came from a deep and raspy voice. Only two words filled the air.

"I know."

2

Unconditional Love: Part II

The touch of death pierced Emma's skin and the words *I know* ran through her like a cold chill down her spine.

"I know," the voice repeated.

Emma opened her eyes and saw complete darkness. Like the cold of the demon's touch, this was a darkness Emma couldn't experience in life. With eyes wide open, Emma couldn't see her hands or anything else discernable. It was complete and utter darkness.

With her eyes failing her, Emma yelled, "What do you know?"

A light brighter than the sun flashed before Emma. She covered her eyes but the light still shone through. Slowly the intensity faded enough for Emma to remove her hands, and as the light continued to dim, Emma slowly began to open her eyes and found herself standing in her home. Not the one she just bought, but the one she started a family in. It was the one she and Jonathan bought just after she found out she was pregnant with Ashley.

It too was a fixer-upper, but it was home. Emma was standing in her bedroom. The queen bed was neatly made but the dresser was a mess. Bottles, bills, brushes, clothes, and more littered the top. Emma looked down at the old shag carpet and jumped when seeing a pair of feet nestled between hers. She rushed to the other side of the room, turned, and looked back. A woman sat on the floor with her back resting against the door. The woman wasn't just anyone... it was her.

"No. No. No." Emma started to cry. "Not here. Not now."

Emma walked to the door, turned the knob, and pulled, but the door didn't budge. It didn't move because a version of her was sitting on the floor. No, it didn't move at all. The door might as well have been part of the wall. Emma tried again and it was the same.

Emma slammed her fist on the door and yelled, "Let me out!" She did this three times before giving up. Emma walked over and sat on the bed. "Please, let me go. I didn't know."

Suddenly a snap rang out and both Emmas looked up. It was the unmistakable sound of Jonathan's belt. He clutched the ends, scrunched up the leather, and jerked it straight, creating the snapping sound, like a bullwhip. The sound was like thunder, warning you that a storm was approaching. The nob on the door jiggled.

"Open the door!" he yelled.

His first pounded on the door and Emma's body jolted with

each smash. When unable to get in, the snapping proceeded until Emma heard Ashley's cries.

"Stop! Please Stop!"

Suddenly Emma was no longer standing in the bedroom but was now in the kitchen. She rushed over to the back door and saw herself getting out of the car.

"No. Please. No," Emma pleaded, but the scene didn't stop unfolding.

The snap of leather started again. Emma could hear Ashley crying and the keys jingling as they unlocked the door. Emma's younger self opened the door and stepped into the house. The belt snapped once more and Emma's head jerked up. She paused until she heard the next snap and then quietly and slowly backed out of the house. Emma watched as she got back into the car and pulled away.

"Please stop. I'm sorry."

Once more Emma's pleas went unheard, and again she was transported. This time she was the passenger in their car; Jonathan was driving while Ashley and Brittany were quietly sitting in the back seat. The silence was out of sheer terror. Ashley gripped her sister's hand tightly as the car haphazardly drove down the worn-out dirt road.

Emma knew this was the end of the road for Jonathan, and each bump made the pit in her stomach grow larger and larger. She looked back at the girls and could tell they wanted to cry, but Emma, like the girls, knew that would only make things worse. Ashley looked over at her sister who stared straight ahead. Tears were pooling in the corners of her eyes but Brittany's strength was holding them back. They had a strength that Emma didn't, and at that moment the shame for all they let Jonathan get away with floated to the surface.

Unable to hold it in any longer, tears flowed as the car came to a halt. Everyone got out of the car and Emma's eyes latched onto Jonathan's. His almost black eyes gleamed with anger and delight. Emma never knew what made one of the kindest souls she ever met turn into Mr. Hyde. However, she realized whatever it was that caused him to turn into a vile person was the same thing that caused her to become a coward.

Without being told, Ashley and Brittany walked to the trunk of the car. This reaction was only the cause of having to do this time and time again. *How many times did he do this?* Emma thought. The snap of the belt brought Emma back to her current reality.

"Bend over," Jonathan ordered.

Ashley did as she was told and Emma saw her eyes lock on the crowbar. She reached out and gripped it so tightly her knuckles turned white. Ashley turned toward Jonathan and swung the iron. It connected with his jaw, the force causing Jonathan's face to turn to the other side of his body. Blood, teeth, and spit spewed from his mouth.

He fell to the ground and Ashley quickly jumped on top of his chest. Before he could react, she reared back her arm and swung. The crunch of Jonathon's jaw breaking made Emma flinch. Like a tennis player returning a volley, Ashley pulled the crowbar across her body and delivered a backhand swing to her father's other jaw.

Blood poured from his mouth, flying all over Ashley as he begged, "Please stop."

The request infuriated Ashley more and she started to swing violently and haphazardly. She hit his head, neck, and shoulders. Emma could tell Ashley just wanted to inflict the same pain he had caused her over all the years.

"That's enough," a raspy voice said.

Ashley jumped off her father and turned to the voice. Emma looked over and saw the demon that terrorized them. Brittany rushed to Ashley's side and they took several steps back from their father and the demon.

"What are you? What do you want?" Ashley demanded.

"I've come for your sin," it answered.

"Take him! He's the one who's sinned. Take him," Ashley screamed.

The black figure waved its finger. "He's not mine to take. Another handles those like him."

The demon turned to his right and another suddenly became visible. It was as if Emma was looking at demonic twins—even the way they moved was the same. The newly appeared one waved its hand and a figure started to become visible. Her husband came into full view despite his body lying just feet before them. Before Jonathan's spirit could react, the demon grabbed Jonathan by the back of his neck. Its mouth moved as if he were saying a thousand words a minute, but nothing came out.

"We all have a job, and mine is to collect you."

Emma was once again transported, and this time she arrived at her new house. All the events that happened from the time they moved in until the time the demon took her flashed before her eyes. When the journey ended, she was face to face with the girls.

"Brittany. Ashley. It's over." Emma tried to move but she couldn't. "What's happening?"

"Why didn't you do anything?" Ashley asked.

"I—I'm so sorry. Please forgive me," Emma pleaded.

"I tried, but I can't. Erlik showed us every opportunity you had to stop it. To do something." Tears flowed down Emma's cheeks. "It's a little late for tears."

"Dad hurt us over and over and you didn't do anything." Brittany wiped a tear from her eye. "You even chose to leave instead of helping us. You deserve punishment as much as he did."

"It's true that he doesn't like children, so we made a deal," Ashley informed.

"What deal?"

"He comes for sins and yours is just as bad as mine, so I offered you."

Emma shook her head. "You offered me?"

"I wanted you to think that you offered yourself as a sacrifice. I wanted you to believe that you were looking after us, and once you felt you did the right thing, I wanted to rip it from you."

"You mean—"

"I'm not done," Ashley interrupted. "Erlik can make you see whatever he wants you to see. We knew the lights were going to turn off and on."

"And he made it look like we were beaten," Brittany added.

"And he made it look like we disappeared when we were beside you the whole time. We saw how panicked you were, but trust me when I say that it was nothing like what we experienced. The longing for your kids to return is nothing like the dread I felt hearing the snap of the belt come closer and closer."

"They suffered and now you must." Erlik appeared from behind the girls. He removed his mask and started walking toward Emma.

"Girls, please don't do this!"

Erlik placed the mask on Emma's face and it attached itself to her like a predator latching on to its pretty. It formed all around her head and only exposed her eyes. Emma's screams, though muffled, were heard.

Ashley and Brittany watched as their mom and Erlik faded away.

3

The Peyton Randolph House: Virginia

"Welcome to Colonial Williamsburg," the tour guide announced. "You may have heard that seeing is believing, but here one must believe to see."

"I believe you're crazy if you believe in nonsense," Jackson whispered to his sister.

"Shhh," Julia replied. "This is going to be great."

He rolled his eyes and began to follow his parents as the guide mumbled on.

"If one is lucky while taking a late-night stroll, they may see shadows dancing past the windows or quickly moving away like a child trying not to get caught looking outside. Sometimes one can see dim yellow lights traveling up a staircase, like a candle guiding one to bed."

"Any of the houses, or are there specific ones?" Robert, Jackson's dad, asked.

Embarrassed, Jackson slowed his pace, and hunched his shoulders, trying to make himself as small as he could.

"Good question," the guide stated. "These events can be seen in many of the homes and buildings around here, but the most disturbing activity happens here."

The guide spread his arms wide, and behind him was a reddish-brown, two-story building with six windows on each wing and one above the door. There were enough windows to see much of the inside of the front of the house, but peering in led Jackson to wonder who or what was looking back. Jackson was skeptical of this whole Ghost Walk from the start, but this house suddenly made him a believer.

A cold chill ran down Jackson's neck, causing him to shake. There was no sign of anyone in the building, but something felt wrong. It felt as though he was being watched. A sudden nudge on his arm woke him from his trance. He looked over to see Julia's elbow retreating to her side and she pointed towards the guide like a teacher on a field trip wanting him to pay attention.

"Welcome to the Peyton Randolph house. Built in 1715, the home grew over the years, and even by today's standards, it is a sizable estate. However, the larger the home the greater the tragedy." The guide grinned like a jack-o'-lantern and stared daggers through Jackson. "There are claims that this house is the most haunted of all places in the United States, which may be true, but only you can decide if that is the case or not."

The chill still clung to Jackson and he no longer wanted to go inside, but the tour was moving on. He quickly scurried in line between his parents and his sister. Jackson's family was behind the other two families in the group, which meant they entered the house last.

Good. If there is something in there it will get the others first, Jackson thought.

As Jackson crossed the threshold, he felt two hands rest on his shoulder, as if someone were trying to remove his jacket. Thinking it was his sister, Jackson quickly jerked his arm back but he didn't hit his sister, just air. He turned to see her a few steps outside of the house looking at her phone.

"Did you do that?" Jackson asked.

"Do what?" Julia snapped. She then stepped forward, brushed by Jackson, and entered the house.

A bad feeling overcame Jackson and his stomach began to twist into knots. He took one more step into the house and a force, like that of a hand, hit him in the chest. Jackson stumbled backward, causing a commotion of thuds from his feet pounding on the floor and hands slapping at the doorframe.

Regaining his footing and standing just outside the door, Jackson said, "I don't think I'm wanted here."

Robert rushed over to Jackson, and though he pleaded with his father not to go in, Jackson was forced to continue the tour. With each step into the house, Jackson felt sicker and sicker. He looked pale and the fright on his face was noticeable, even to Julia.

"What's wrong?" she asked.

"This place. There's something here. It pushed me out the door and I got this weird knot in my stomach."

"Thank god. I thought it was just me. This place gives me

the creeps too." Julia grabbed Jackson's hand. "Come on. Stay close to me."

Jackson didn't argue and immediately latched onto his sister.

"I will warn you all that we are about to go up the stairs to the second floor, and I urge you to keep one hand on the railing at all times. Guests tend to experience a bit of vertigo when they let go of the railing and become off-balanced."

Julia and Jackson were the last to ascend the stairs. They held onto the rail with their right arm and Julia's left trailed behind her as she held Jackson's hand. All was well as they made it to the first turn. They made it three more steps when Julia's jacket pocket began to buzz. Removing her hand from the railing, she reached into her pocket to see an incoming text.

The light of the home screen flickered like it was shorting out. Julia looked up and a young girl, maybe eight or nine years old, wearing a white dress smiled and lunged at her. The cold hands hit her chest and Julia started to fall backward. Jackson held up his hands and prevented her from tumbling down.

"Julia!" their mother yelled.

Their parents rushed down the stairs and helped them up. When she told them what happened, they blamed it on her letting go of the rail, not because of a vengeful spirit. They helped Julia up the stairs and the tour continued. With each room toured, Julia and Jackson saw shadows of two children following them. They heard the creaking of the floorboards from rooms with no one in them, but thankfully Jackson and Julia only saw and heard things for the remainder of the tour. Nothing physically harmed them again.

The tour was finally coming to an end and they exited

the house with no one else experiencing an encounter. Before they moved on to their next stop, the tour guide gathered the group around so they could take pictures one last time. Everyone pulled out their phones and began snapping away. Everyone except Jackson and Julia. They were frozen in place, staring at the window to the right of the front door.

A hooded figure rested behind the panes of glass. One could only see the shoulders, the hood surrounding a head, and a face. The face lacked discernable features. It was almost like a skeleton, but its eyes were black as night, blacker than the hood surrounding the white bone cheeks.

Just when Julia and Jackson thought they were the only ones seeing the ghost, a woman screamed, "He's in the window! I told you we weren't alone!"

4

The Jersey Devil: Part I

"Greetings fellow Corkonians, and welcome back to another episode of The Corky Files. I'm your host J.D. but you can call me Jay. In addition to broadcasting to your chosen device, I'm also streaming via CorkyFiles.com where you can ask questions and submit your feedback.

"Now that the introduction is over, it's with great sadness that I report the passing of local spook show legend Crazy Carl. Carl Clarkson was given the nickname Crazy Carl after claiming to have spotted Bigfoot in the late 70s and then again in 1982. From then on, he continued to see the infamous and elusive creature every other year. Why he never carried a camera is beyond me. Carl also claimed to not only have seen aliens but was abducted at least twice. He did confess that the third and fourth incidents could have been a dream. Carl started his radio show in the early 90s and kept all of us up to date on what he called, 'all things weird and not of this earth.' He inspired me to create this podcast, and so I say to Carl, wherever you may be, thank you for the inspiration. I hope you've found the truth you were always searching for.

"Now that the emotional things are out of the way, I'd like to remind everyone that this year is the Year of the Devil. In honor of the spirit of Carl, I'm going to read his notes from 1993."

October 25th, 1993:

I saw him! I saw the Devil walking on my ride home. It was 9:43 p.m. and I just turned onto 2nd Street when I locked eyes with the Devil himself. Its eyes were as red as a fire engine and had black, soul-piercing centers. It only lasted a second, and then it sprinted away. I gave chase but it was fast, too fast for me. I will continue to patrol the streets to see if I can see The Devil once more.

October 26th, 1993:

I woke up this morning to hear that Timmy Robinson had disappeared in the middle of the night. He's just fourteen and his parents said they last saw him at 10:30. He was staying up late to finish a project, and when his parents woke, Timmy was nowhere to be found. I've gathered all the information available and there are no signs of foul play. All accounts point to him leaving on his own but nothing can be verified.

I did my patrol and I couldn't find any sign of the beast lurking on our streets. Did poor Timmy satisfy its sick twisted needs?

October 27th, 1993:

I heard the most chilling and blood-curdling scream in my life tonight. It was 10:30 p.m. when I heard this...this...scream to end all screams. Just the thought of it causes a chill to run down my spine. I know that of all the things that have happened to me in my life, that scream will be the one thing that forever haunts me.

I rushed toward the sound as fast as I could, turning onto Cleveland Avenue, and there it was. But it wasn't alone. And it was different this time. It was dragging a body in each arm.

I shouted, "Let them go!"

It turned, and once more I saw those red eyes. This time it had horns protruding from its head. They were small, and they weren't there yesterday, but they were definitely horns. The Devil pulled up the bodies and ran off. I gave chase and saw it turn onto Carter's Ally. When I got there, it and the bodies were gone. It was as though he vanished into thin air.

I went to the police station to file a report but they laughed at me and proclaimed, "Crazy Carl strikes again."

October 28th, 1993:

I woke to the commotion of everyone scurrying about the street. A county-wide search party had been called to look for the Moore twins, Amber and Tiffany. That's who it took last night. Three kids in three nights is too much of a coincidence.

I ran back to the police station and they took my report seriously this time. However, they still didn't call it The Devil. They said to be on the lookout for "a man wearing different masks. One with horns and one without."

I don't know why they won't believe me. The records speak for themselves. The Devil comes every thirty years and takes seven kids. The county newspapers have the reports but no one is paying attention. No one will listen to me!

Despite not believing me, I still helped look for the kids.

October 29th, 1993:

We searched for the kids well into the night, and nothing. Not a single clue about where they went. The cops examined Carter's Alley and there was nothing. The only good news is that no kids were taken last night. The bad news is that Scott Adams disappeared between 9:00 p.m. and 10:30 p.m..

It's currently 11:00 p.m..

I didn't do my patrol tonight.

I failed Scott.

October 30th, 1993:

Tonight was the high school's Halloween Dance, and two kids on their way home never made it. Nichole Fisher and Jeremy Parker left the dance but never made it to their respective homes. Jeremy's car was found in a ditch just off Route 780 three miles from Nichole's house. The conditions of the grass, dirt, and mud should have shown signs of them leaving the car, but not a trace of evidence of their exiting the vehicle was found.

The cops and search dogs scoured the area, but everyone turned up empty-handed. How could they exit the car without leaving a trace? How could the dogs not pick up a scent? I know The Devil is responsible but I don't know how he's doing this.

I was in town doing my patrol when this all happened. We're now up to six kids.

One day and one victim left.

October 31st, 1993:

The town was on high alert today. I was at the grocer and heard many families planning on sleeping in the same room so that no one could vanish without knowing what happened. J.J.'s gun shop had a line that stretched for two blocks. I drove by later and saw that he placed a sign stating one box of ammo per gun per customer.

I made my patrol but saw nothing. Not a shadow out of place. No red, beady eyes. However, I'm not surprised. Cops with community volunteers patrolled the streets with such efficiency that it would be hard to commit an act such as abduction. My theory is that since everyone is on such high alert, The Devil is watching and plotting. I just pray that we can catch him or at least prevent another one of our youth from disappearing.

November 1st, 1993:

I got home too late last night to finish writing. I gave my report to the officers but once more they didn't believe me. To be honest, I'm not even sure I believe it myself. For hours I rode around Cork and nothing was happening, but something told me to check the cemetery. I'm not sure how to explain the feeling...but I knew I had to go check.

When I arrived at the front gate, the hairs on my neck stood up. I got the creepiest feeling that I've ever gotten. Something wasn't right. I pulled out my flashlight from my bag and proceeded with caution. I kept walking until I got to the back gates...to Settler's Lot. My heart started to race and sweat poured from my face. My hand shook as I opened the gate. It was undoubtedly the most scared I've ever been in my life.

I entered and proceeded to creep further and further until I heard deep breaths. I turned off my flashlight and slowly walked in that direction. I began to see a white glow outlining a mass. It was a body, but it was larger than any human one I'd ever seen. It was big, like Andre the Giant big. I could also see horns, but not the numbs I witnessed the other day. No, these were full-grown horns like that of an adult ram.

Suddenly, the area lit up and I could see the bodies. Each one of the kids that had been taken was lying on the ground. I gasped and complete darkness returned. The Devil turned to me and I immediately ran. I must have fallen a dozen times before I got out of the cemetery, but eventually, I got out. When I brought the police back to Settler's Lot, we didn't find The Devil or the children. But we did find an outline of them. It was like their bodies were burned into the ground.

I still don't know who the last victim was yet, but I'm sure I'll find out soon.

"That was the last entry from Carl's journal relating to The Devil. The last victim was Devin Turner, and beyond the disappearance of the victims, no one can say for certain how true this story is. I checked with members of our community who were alive back then, and everyone assumed they were dealing with some sort of serial kidnapper. They mentioned that the national headlines were full of stories about kidnappings and other warnings like checking candy for razor blades. When I mentioned the Jersey Devil, I was met with a laugh. Everyone pretty much brushed that theory off as a story parents told children to keep them in line and nothing more.

"So what do you think? Type in your questions or comments and I'll spend the next couple of minutes answering them as best as I can."

Jay turned his head to the computer monitor and read, "JustInCaseIForget asks: Can we call you Crazy Jay now? That's a great question, and it would be an honor to be called that. Also, I want everyone to know that JustInCaseIForget is one of my best friends and also a jackass." Jay looked for the next question.

"WonderingAlice asks: Why do you think Settler's Lot was where this happened? That's a great question and I believe it's because of the seclusion. The majority of our homes are town-centered, and thus more areas to be spotted. Even on the edge of town, we have well-lit streets due to the Street Light statute of 1975 as a result of the fiery car crash. We do have some back roads leading to the farms of the county, but for the most part, the cemetery is the prime location to take someone to. It's close to town, but not too far where it's difficult to take someone.

"It closes before nightfall, lacks lighting past the main sidewalk, and Settler's Lot is on the far edge of the cemetery. It has an old stone wall that rises four feet off the ground and woods that border the backside. It would be a perfect spot to commit atrocities. Great question WonderingAlice."

"BIGTom asks: Why are you bringing up this tragedy? They were our friends and family. Well, first off BIGTom, I'm sorry for your loss. I'm not trying to hurt anyone here but I'm hoping to remind my friends of what I believe awaits us this month. I believe that this story is true, and we need to be prepared. We have little time, and I urge everyone to place locators on their children's phones, place a tracking tag in their backpacks, and keep an eye on their security cameras. I pray that I'm wrong but I've done the research. I read the accounts since the first happenings. What happened in 1993 happened many times before.

"I think that is enough questions for today, so in the memory of Carl, 'Stay safe and stay aware. This is Jay and The Corky Files signing off."

Jay's phone immediately rang and he answered, "Crazy Jay."

"Dude, why did you do all of that?" Justin yelled.

"All of what?"

"The episode was so wrong. Those victims still have family here and some are still messed up over it."

"I swear I didn't mean any harm by it, but I got this bad feeling. Something is telling me that we're not safe."

"You hung out with Carl too much."

"He's a legend, but that's not it. Do you know that feeling you get when you get called to the principal's office?"

"You mean the feeling that your heart is falling into the pit of your stomach and hope ceases to exist? While you make the long walk to the office, your stomach is in knots and a cold chill runs over you that makes the hair stand up on your neck. As your mind races, the thought of being haunted by a ghost is comforting compared to the thought of the principal calling your mom."

"Exactly. That's what I'm feeling. Something is just telling me that The Jersey Devil isn't a bedtime story. I think he's real and he's coming for us."

5

The Jersey Devil: Part II

"Okay," Justin said.

"Okay, what?" Jay asked.

"I'm in."

"But you don't even know what you're in for."

"Doesn't matter. That was the most real moment I've ever had with you. I've never heard you that serious, and if you're that serious, then I got your back."

"Thanks."

"You're welcome, but what are we going to do?"

"I'm working on a plan but we have to wait until the twenty-fifth."

"Greetings fellow Corkonians and welcome to a special

morning episode of The Corky Files. I'm your host J.D. but you can call me Jay. Due to class starting in less than an hour, I will be brief.

"Today, as you know, is October twenty-fourth, the day before The Devil is to strike. I encourage you to make sure your doors and windows are locked. Don't go out alone and be home before dark. Remember The Devil is known for targeting those between the ages of twelve and seventeen. Be safe."

Jay ended the broadcast and went to school. The walk was short but he couldn't help asking himself, *Who's he going to take tonight?* Each student he passed was a potential victim and each one glared at him. Their squinty eyes, clenched jaws, and shaking heads left no doubt that he was public enemy number one.

Things didn't change as the clock ticked away. During class changes, students moved away from Jay as he passed; they'd stop mid-sentence to stare, or go from a normal tone to a whisper as he approached. Some slammed their lockers in either an attempt to display their anger or to give him as much of a fright as he was giving them.

Lunch came around and the only ones who acknowledged Jay were his crew—the ones who accepted him for all his quirks. Though they may not like the podcast, they were supportive of him.

He walked to the table, and before he could sit down Jessica informed, "Dude, you're seriously the new Crazy Carl."

Jay looked around and it seemed like all eyes were on him. Those sitting at the table were looking in his direction and people in the lunch line were doing the same. The line moved at a snail's pace and all eyes were locked on him.

"I think you're right." Jay sat down and pulled out his lunch from his backpack. He looked around at his friends. "Are you sure it's okay for me to sit here? I don't mind backing off for a few days."

Jamie's mouth was full of half his Twinkie, but he mumbled, "We're already outcasts, so what does it matter?"

"We're not outcasts," Jay insisted.

April held up a finger. "We're freshmen." She held us a second. "Podcaster of the supernatural." A third finger. "Friends of the podcaster."

Samantha elbowed April. "It's no biggie. I mean what if you're right? How are we going to stop it?"

"Yeah," Justin said. "I've been wondering that myself. I mean, Crazy Carl couldn't do anything. Kids older than us couldn't be kept from being taken, and it seemed like this thing managed to avoid an entire town on patrol."

"I've been thinking about that, and what we need is a sleep-over." Jay took a large bite of his sandwich.

April shook her head. "My parents won't go for it."

"Why not? We used to sleep over at each other's house all the time," Samantha explained.

April motioned from her head down her body. "That's when we were little. Things have changed."

"Ah, puberty. Such a heartless—"

"But," Jay interrupted. Unable to finish, Justin immediately went into puppy-dog-face mode. "My parents are okay with it. The girls will stay in my sister's room and the guys with me."

"My parents should be okay with that...I think," April said.

"You know what's not okay?" Terrance asked.

Jay turned and looked up. Terrance was a foot taller than him while standing up, but even while seated, he took on the form of a Giant. Terrance was like a lion hunting a rabbit.

"Look Ter—"

"Shut it. We got a lot going on this week. If you keep running your mouth and something happens, then everything will get canceled. No games, no parties, and no fun."

"You're going to get us sent back to the dial-up days," Seth, one of Terrance's minions, added.

Jay started to stand and Terrance shoved him back to his seat. "No more Devil talk. It's just a stupid story parents tell to keep us scared and in line. Talk about it one more time and you'll find it hard to talk at all."

Jay watched Terrance, Seth, and the rest of the minions head to their table. He then turned back to his friends.

"Are you going to be okay until the end of school?" Jamie asked.

"Well, if The Devil doesn't get me then Terrance will." Jay was met with blank stars. "I won't go on air and talk about it until something happens."

"Let's hope nothing will," April noted.

"Let's hope Terrance is victim number one and his cronies fill up the rest of the slots." Samantha looked up from her wrap. Everyone's mouth was open and they were shaking their heads. "What? I can be mean too. Lots of dark thoughts roll around my head ya know."

"Just when you think you know everything about someone you've known since birth." Justin motioned that his head was exploding. "They drop a bomb."

"Oh sweetie, the bomb isn't me telling you I have dark thoughts. That would be me telling you what they are." Samantha smirked.

After the laughing subsided, Jamie cleared his throat. "Let's talk snack situation."

October 25th, 2023:

The doorbell rang and Jay opened the app to see who was at the door. The crew was all there with bags and backpacks.

He pressed the talk button and announced, "Drop your stuff off in the living room and head to my office in the basement."

"When did he get an office?" Justin asked.

"It's their old storage room," Jamie answered.

"I can still hear you." Everyone looked at the camera. "It's an office."

Jay could hear the pounding of feet on the stairs as he waited for his friends to see what he'd done.

Justin threw open the door and stormed in. "There's no way—"

Jay was standing with his arms in the air and announced, "Welcome to the War Room!"

The room was decorated with newspaper articles, drawings, and printed pages. There were two boards on easels. They looked just like the walls but numbers were scattered about the boards.

"I can't believe your parents let you do this," April said.

"Yeah, I hate to say this, but you're looking like Crazy Carl right now," Samantha added.

"What is this?" Jamie asked.

"I know it all looks crazy, but it's all research. Most of it's mine but some of it's from Carl. He enjoyed the hunt more than sitting in front of a computer or looking through town archives."

"What's his and what's yours?" Justin asked.

"The sketches are pretty much all done by Carl except for any that look printed from the internet or copied from a book. The rest is pretty much all me."

"That's like..." April looked around the room. "Almost all of it. You mean you've pretty much done all of this?"

Jay shrugged his shoulders. "I couldn't—"

Jay stopped and all eyes were on him. He scanned the room and looked at each one of his friends. They all had known each other for as long as they could remember. They weren't just his friends but his family. He didn't want to tell them his real feelings but knew he must.

Samantha walked over to Jay and began rubbing his back. "Are you okay?"

Jay nodded. "I know I believe in weird stuff, but I've done the research for two years now and I'm telling you it's real. I got so obsessed with all of it not because of loving *the weird* but because I love *you guys*. We're in the target age group and I can't lose any of you."

No one spoke, but everyone looked at each other. It was like Jay dropped a bomb. Their looks were a mix of fear and sadness. Despite Jay wanting them together for their safety, he could tell that none of them had thought they could be on The Devil's list.

"Well, crap," Jamie said. When all eyes were on him, he explained, "We have to help him now. He brought feelings and stuff into this."

The doorbell chimed again and Jay pulled out his phone. "Dinner is here. It's on me tonight."

"Just tonight?" Jamie asked.

"Yep, I just used the rest of my birthday money to feed us so everyone's pitching in tomorrow."

"Wait? Tomorrow?" Samantha asked.

"Yep. I'll explain everything after dinner."

6

The Jersey Devil: Part III

Jay looked around at the lack of chairs in his office. "Are you okay with sitting on the floor?"

"That's fine, but don't blame me if I fall asleep," April said.

Jamie yawned. "Yeah, I think I ate too much."

"You'll fine be," Jay insisted. "Now, we've all heard the stories of The Devil. Some believe it's a winged creature and others believe it to be half-human and half-goat. Carl's account states it had horns that got bigger. I believe Carl's account, but I don't believe it's demonic."

"How could a half-human and half-goat not be demonic?" Jamie interrupted.

"So, I think this is a person who's being used as a vessel of sorts, or a deal's been made with one."

Like she was in class, Samantha raised her hand and asked, "Why do we call it 'The Devil' when it may just be a person?"

April pointed to Samantha. "That's a great question. Why use the term Devil when we aren't certain it's the Devil?"

"We're getting a little off topic but whatever. I believe it's because of the time and the people. The late 1600s were the height of the Salem Witch Trials, and if something bad was happening, then the Devil was to blame. Much easier to say the Devil made them do it than try to find out the name of the demon. Of course, the majority of those accused who perished or suffered any sort of punishment were innocent of witchcraft. Those who were guilty probably committed the crimes more so because of their sick and twisted desires instead of possession. Now, all of this leads us to the identity of The Devil."

"What!" Justin yelled. "You know who The Devil is?"

"Shhh, and yes. Carl said the last place he saw The Devil was at Settler's Lot, but Carl couldn't remember where exactly. He said that between the darkness and the fright, he couldn't remember where he was. Since he couldn't remember, I began researching the plots. There had to be a reason The Devil was at Settler's Lot."

Samantha raised her hand and said, "I thought you said it was due to location. You know, it's secluded."

"I had to say that on the show. The truth is he went there because he has a connection—"

"It's his resting spot!" Jamie shouted.

Jay snapped his fingers. "Exactly. I noted and researched every plot. There are five rows at the edge of Settler's Lot reserved for those deemed unworthy. Each row has dozens of graves for those called 'The Damned.' The area was used as a cautionary tale after Sunday service. I found several accounts where families would walk in a line, like a parade, to *The Damned* and tell the kids some sort of story of terror."

April, following Samantha's lead, raised her hand and asked, "You're joking, right?"

"I'm as serious as my belief in The Devil. Now, the stories told were different, made up, true, or somewhere in between. I never really found an account stating what was said so I added that part myself. I think it's safe to say that they told whatever they thought would scare their kids." Jay held up a finger. "In their defense, the stories of those buried are pretty brutal. I mean, some are like wild-west vile." Jay walked over and grabbed a picture from his desk. He held up a picture of a worn-out tombstone. "Former Suspect number 10, Tombstone Marker 178. The true name of Marker 178 is unknown and I dug extensively to try and find it but got nothing. He was considered so wicked that the powers of the time struck his name from all records in hopes his sins would be buried with him. I found one journal entry that said he killed thirty-five, robbed and injured a dozen more, raped an undisclosed amount, burned down the church, kidnapped and sold a dozen kids, was found eating his last victim, and the last of it just said, 'amongst other atrocities.' It was noted that his trial lasted thirty minutes and he was hung almost immediately after."

"Why isn't he suspect number one?" April asked.

"Because what's happening is personal. Marker 178 died knowing and accepting his guilt, so coming back wouldn't occur in this pattern. Someone like 178 would never leave and nothing would fill his bloodlust. No, what's happening in Cork only occurs every thirty years and only happens to seven people between the ages of twelve and seventeen."

Without raising his hand, Justin asked, "Why every thirty years, and why that age range?"

"The first incident of children being taken occurred in 1723, and all between the ages of twelve and seventeen, and all in the last week of October. Nothing happened again for another thirty years, then another thirty, and so on. So I decided to back up thirty years to October of 1693. The famous witch trials in Salem were over but you must keep in mind that Cork was a deeply religious county. From its founding in 1674 to 1693, people came in droves because this became known as '*The Town of Truths*' and the leader of witch trials, convictions, and deaths in the colonies.

"If one suspected a family member of ill-doings but had no proof, then this town would reveal all. You see, it was here where they believed one would become either closer to their faith or to temptation. The only problem was that Cork attracted not just the religious but also the infamous. Criminals flocked here in hopes of exploiting the situation and what ensued was chaos that culminated in October of 1693."

"Finally we get to the story." Jamie yawned and was met with a face full of April's pillow.

"I found that three people were hung on October 31st." Jay grabbed three pictures and passed them around. "John Ackley, Robert Hays, and George Backlee. George was a real scum of the earth type and guilty to the core. John and Robert were the best of friends and had just finished a late night out at The King's Tavern. They had too much to drink and John told Robert to sleep it off at his house. Robert lived on the outskirts of the county and was in no shape to ride, so he agreed. So, they stumbled into John's house and woke to the most horrific of all screams.

"John and Robert woke to see bloody bodies all around them and George Backlee rising to his feet. The only thing John was certain of was that this wasn't his house and a wound on his head meant there was some sort of fight. All three were arrested and testimonies from witnesses were quickly given. Seven witnesses in total who ranged from twelve to seventeen claimed they were drawn to the Mattox house by the spell cast by John, Robert, and George. Each stated they saw them drinking the blood of the Mattox family and chanting in some foreign tongue.

"They were given as fair of a trial that someone accused of witchcraft could be given, but the events were somewhat shocking. George told the court, 'Go ahead and hang me,' and never spoke again. John gave his testimony and stuck to their innocence but Robert rolled over and admitted to everything. One account said that the priest coerced Robert to spare his family name and that admittance would wipe his sin away. John was devastated and held onto his innocence. All three were convicted of murder and were declared to be in cahoots with the Devil. The hanging was set on October 31st."

"So it's either John or Robert, right?" April asked. "I mean if this account is true about John and Robert going home, then they stumbled into the Mattox house while George was killing the family. Maybe a struggle broke out and somehow all three got knocked unconscious or they knocked George out and passed out from drinking."

Samantha butted in, "Yeah, and George was guilty so he

wouldn't come back. Robert was told that his sins would be gone if he confessed, the pearly gates waiting for him. John was sure to have felt betrayed and must have a reason to come back."

"Ya'll know how to ruin the flow of a story. But yes, I believe it's John not because he was betrayed but because of what happened to him after the trial. The Mattox family was a pillar of the community and people wanted the killers to suffer. However, John holding tight to his innocence didn't sit well with the community. Every night the prison guards would take a break and members of the community would spend hours torturing him. He was flogged and beaten, and he suffered the colonial form of waterboarding. By the time of his hanging, John was nearly dead, but his last words are as follows:

'Today you hang two innocent men, but after tonight I will no longer maintain my innocence. I will find a way to come back and take from you what you hold dear.'

"So there we have it, the who." Jay took a bow.

"And the why," Justin added.

"But what about the when and why the teen victims?" Jamie asked.

"I think the when has something to do with his age. John was thirty years old when he died, but the teens are for two reasons. One is because they lied and two is because children tend to be what parents hold most dear."

Samantha raised her hand. "Why seven?"

"At first, I thought it was due to the number of accusers, but I didn't have proof. I searched and searched but I couldn't find anything definitive so I talked to Mrs. Kelly—"

"The school librarian?" Everyone looked at Justin. "What? I

read…on occasion." Justin cleared his throat. "Why would you go to the library?"

"Where else would you go for answers?" Justin pointed to his phone. "Mrs. Kelly was a senior in high school the last time The Devil came and I think I know why the taken were chosen."

7

The Jersey Devil: Part IV

Interviewing Mrs. Kelly (Past):

"What can I do for you, Jay?"

Mrs. Kelly was her usual perky and happy self. She never failed to greet him with a smile. It was just one of the many things that made her his favorite teacher at the school. Of course, her lack of judgment was at the top of the list too.

"Well, I've done some research and I need some help."

"You've come to the right place." She moved a stack of books to the side and replaced them with her keyboard. "Where should we start?"

Jay pulled out a folder from his backpack and placed it on the counter. "I know this isn't going to be easy, but I was wondering if you could shed some light on some of your old classmates."

Mrs. Kelly opened the folder and moved through the seven

pictures. The smile from the always-happy Mrs. Kelly faded and her face became grim. Her eyes glazed over, her lips quivered, and her hands caressed the pictures like they were priceless artifacts.

"Jay, I can't."

"I wouldn't ask if it wasn't important. I think—I know what happened to them is going to happen again."

"What happened was a tragic one-time thing—"

"Mrs. Kelly, please. If nothing happens, then great. I'm just another fool who got tricked into chasing an urban legend. But if I'm right, then more of the students here will meet the same fate."

Mrs. Kelly took a deep breath, turned, and waved. "Come on."

Jay followed Mrs. Kelly into her office and took a seat across from her desk. She closed the door and took a seat. Sitting behind her desk, Mrs. Kelly was as still as a statue.

Jay cleared his throat. "Thanks for doing this."

"What do you want to know?" she almost whispered.

Jay opened the folder and handed over the first picture. "What was he like?"

Mrs. Kelly grabbed the picture. "Timmy Robinson was...a good kid. I mean, sure he had his faults. What teen doesn't?"

Jay had just pulled out his notepad and pen. He clicked on the pen and asked, "What was Timmy's fault?"

"He was highly skilled at taking things that weren't his. The funny thing is that his family was extremely wealthy and Timmy could buy anything he wanted, but the classic five-finger discount was appealing. He never stole wallets, valuables, or anything that could get him into real trouble. Timmy solely took things that didn't matter, like candy, but he would resell them at school."

"The rich get richer," Jay mumbled.

"I'm sorry?"

Jay shook his head. "Nothing. Is that all?"

Mrs. Kelly shrugged her shoulders. "Though we are a small community, it's easy not to know a lot. You should know what more than anyone." Jay nodded. "We all have a group and only know what's on the surface with those not in it."

"I like that and may use it if you don't mind." Jay handed over the next picture. "What about Amber and Tiffany Moore?"

Mrs. Kelly sniffed and turned her head. "I was close to Tiffany; she was like a sister. We were constantly together and always had our noses in a book. Amber was the worst and I mean the worst. I don't think I could find something positive about her if I tried. Though they were twins, one would have never been able to tell. Amber was beautiful." Mrs. Kelly laughed. "Who am I kidding? She was gorgeous. Amber was the most beautiful girl in our grade and arguably the most beautiful in the school. This was not just a common belief for everyone in the school but for Amber as well. Amber knew how attractive she was and constantly reminded Tiffany who got the looks in the family." Mrs. Kelly sighed. "Tiffany was considered the ugly duckling."

"So Tiffany was jealous of her sister?"

"Tiffany was constantly reminded by almost everyone how beautiful her sister was. It tore Tiffany up. She was always on edge around anyone and loved reading so much because it was the only way to escape reality. Tiffany once told me that she wished she could be half as pretty as Amber for just one day. She was tired of people asking, 'Why don't you look like your sister?' or 'I thought you were twins.' I don't know what happened to them, but I do know Amber got what she deserved for the way she treated Tiffany."

"Sounds like it, and I hate to hear what Tiffany went through that." Jay passed over the next picture.

"Ah, Scott Adams. He came from the wealthiest family in Cork. They've moved since the disappearance, but before everything, Scott could be considered the most worthless human being I've ever known. He was waited on hand and foot from the moment he woke up to the moment he went to bed. A butler brought him breakfast in bed, dressed him, cut up his food, and so on. In school, he slept until lunch and he never ate in the cafeteria. His butler brought him his food and he ate out in their car. The only reason he passed a class was that his last name was Adams. I never saw him turn in an assignment, take a test, or do a project, but he somehow managed to pass with straight As."

"Almost makes you wonder why he went to school at all."

"State law," Mrs. Kelly informed.

Jay held up a picture and asked, "What about Nichole?"

"I wasn't close to her but I do know about the cheating scandal."

Jay leaned forward. "Scandal?"

"Nichole was newly single after catching her boyfriend, Jake, cheating on her at a party. She was so angry that she went to Jake's best friend and asked him to the dance. Jeremy didn't hesitate and agreed. Nichole wanted to hurt Jake and the best way was through Jeremy. The two were like brothers, and she knew that being with Jeremy would be the ultimate revenge. Each time Jake saw them together, the knife would dig deeper and deeper. Nichole's end goal wasn't just to hurt Jake but to hurt his bond with Jeremy. Jeremy never realized Nichole's intentions because the only thing on his mind was the impure thoughts of the fun he was going to have." Mrs. Kelly took a deep breath. "Want to know the worst part?" Jay nodded. "Jake never cheated on Nichole. I was at that party."

Jay leaned back in his seat. "I don't mean any offense, but I can't see you at a party."

Mrs. Kelly laughed. "I know and I rarely went, but I did go to that one and saw the entire thing. The other girl came on to Jake and Nichole happened to walk in at that moment. She didn't wait for Jake to pull away and never gave him a chance to explain. It was one of the few occasions where I felt sad for Jake."

"That's terrible," Jay mumbled.

"Not as terrible as what happened to Devin." Jay handed over the last picture. Tears flowed from Mrs. Kelly.

"I'm sorry. We don't have to continue. I think I have all I need."

Mrs. Kelly grabbed a tissue and wiped the tears. "No, it's okay. We've come this far. Devin—Devin was the best. He was the nicest guy to ever walk the earth and would give the shirt off his back to help anyone. His passion was baking and cooking, but it led to an unhealthy lifestyle. Due to being of a larger size, Devin had a hard time fitting in with the guys, so he primarily hung out with me and my friends. Losing him was like losing a brother."

"I'm sorry," Jay comforted.

"Me too." Mrs. Kelly grabbed another tissue.

✳ ✳ ✳

Present

Justin finally followed suit and raised his hand. "I don't get the connection."

"Yeah," Jamie said. "I mean they had their faults but I don't understand."

"But they weren't just faults," Samantha informed. "They were sins."

"Ha! I know a thing or two about sin but they didn't have the chance to finish one," Justin joked.

Rolling her eyes, Samantha continued, "They all committed one of the seven deadly sins. Timmy Robinson was greed, Amber was pride—"

"Tiffany was jealousy," April interjected.

"Or envy," Samantha clarified. "Nicole was wrath, Jeremy had lustful intentions, and Devin was gluttony."

"Exactly!" Jay shouted. "John is going after those deemed most precious to a parent but guilty of sin. By all accounts after his death, John was innocent and though not alive, John won't let an innocent suffer as he did."

"How does he know who sinned?" Jamie asked.

Samantha pointed to Jamie. "That's a good question. I mean, I'm sure you could pick any teen and find something bad they've done but John targeted specific sins."

"I wondered that myself and came across an English monk's journal from the late 1500s. He claimed to have an out-of-body experience where he was a demon. As this demon, he walked the streets just like you or me but he was able to see an aura of a person. Each one was a different color and each one had a distinct smell. He recalled this overwhelming desire to harm certain colors, but he didn't know why at the time. The monk spent some time outside of the monastery finding locals he had the urge to attack. He learned that each one repeatedly violated a sin and assumed that each sin had a color and a distinct smell."

"So, John is a demon now?" Jamie asked.

"Carl said that when he first saw The Devil it was more like a man than a beast. When he saw The Devil at Settler's Lot he was larger and had full-grown horns. I think a demon is using John as a vessel and we need to separate the demon from the man."

"So, how do we do that?" April asked.

"I have a theory, but let's wait until tomorrow and see if The Devil is real. Go grab your stuff and head to your respective room."

October 26, 2023:

The blaring buzz of the radioactive-style alarm came from everyone's cell phone. Jay jumped out of his bed, and if it wasn't for Jamie sitting up seconds before, his foot would have landed dead-center of Jamie's chest.

"Cut it off," Jamie yelled.

"It's an amber alert! I can't," Jay replied.

The alert stopped as quickly as it sounded and was replaced with phones ringing and texts dinging.

Jay answered the phone while the others silenced theirs. He placed it on speaker, and greeted, "Hello."

"Good morning, this is Superintendent Jacklyn Jones. In light of the overnight events, all schools will be closed today and all activities will be canceled. Our thoughts and prayers are going out to our Corky family. In the interest of your safety, we encourage all citizens to go out in pairs and to be in their homes before sundown."

Jay ended the call and looked at messages from texts and social media alerts.

"What happened?" Jamie asked.

"I keep looking and can't find anything." Justin's thumb rapidly moved across his screen. "I think someone's missing but no one knows who."

"Let's see if the girls have heard anything." Jay led the way to his sister's room and knocked on the door. "Can we come in or meet downstairs?"

There was a moment of silence and then the door slowly opened. Jay's sister appeared and the sound of crying could be heard. She waved Jay in and upon entering he saw April rubbing Samantha's back and holding her tight.

"It's Carrie," April informed.

"Oh, Sam. I'm sorry." Jamie sat beside Samantha. "Do you want to talk about it?"

Samantha wiped her face and answered, "I don't even know what to talk about. I woke up and saw a dozen messages from her parents asking if I knew where she was. She's the one missing."

Jay looked into Samantha's eyes. He didn't just see her pain, but her fear, and suddenly it hit him.

The Devil was no longer a cautionary tale, no longer a topic of research, and no longer a podcast episode.

The Devil is real and coming for them.

8

The Jersey Devil: Part V

"Carrie was—" Samantha took a deep breath. "She was envy. Carrie's family works and works but they always struggle. She never wanted more than anyone else, but some of what they had. You, know? Like, she always had to pick buying clothes for school over going out to dinner and a movie. She wanted to be able to go out and get new clothes."

"I didn't realize." April looked mortified. "I wasn't that nice to her."

"Jay." Samantha looked up. "How do we stop it?"

"I can't ask you all to help me."

"You didn't," Samantha informed. "I asked you."

"Yeah, Jay." Jamie stood up. "We've got to try and stop it. I mean, even if we survive, then it's our kids who will have to deal with this next, so let's do what we can to stop it."

"I'm with them," Justin informed.

"Yeah, me too." April nodded.

"Okay, but you all have to realize that we may not make it back. I mean, The Devil may not pick us but he can certainly harm us for trying to stop him." Jay looked at all the nodding heads. "Let's get dressed, eat, and then see Father O'Brian."

Corky Cathedral wasn't much of a cathedral in the traditional sense of a castle-like structure. It was a rectangular brick building that made it look more like a school than a church. Jay and his crew entered the chapel and were almost immediately met by Father O'Brian.

"I don't want to sound rude because it's good to see you children, but you should be at home and not out and about," Father O'Brian informed.

"We need your help," Jay pleaded.

"In times like these, we could use all the help we can get but I'm afraid there isn't much I can do."

"Father, I believe The Jersey Devil is not only real but part demon."

"Part? Do you think it's someone possessed?" Father O'Brian asked.

"No, this goes beyond possession, but we need holy water and the spirit wards."

Jamie cleared his throat. Jay looked back and saw he was raising his hand. "What's a spirit ward?"

The priest answered, "An old tool that monks and priests used to scare off evil spirits, but how do you know I have them?"

"Last year you did a sermon on rebuilding and mentioned that the spirit wards were the only things that survived the 1923 fire. You used it as a symbol of saying how not even the most destructive force can destroy our faith."

"Here I thought you just sat there and jotted down notes for your next podcast," Father O'Brian said.

"Oh, I do that too."

Father O'Brian chucked and waved for them to follow. "You know, I was here the last time this happened."

"Do you believe us or think it's a copycat kidnapper?" Jay asked.

"I believe that you believe it's real, and that's all that matters. You're either going on a hunt to stop something vile from happening or trying to protect yourself, so what kind of priest, or person, would I be if I failed to help?"

Father O'Brian led them to a storage room next to his office. It was filled with everything to tend to the church's needs; office supplies, food, robes, and tools were neatly organized on the shelving units.

"In the back are two trunks that have the spirit wards. I'll get some bottles of holy water and meet you back in the chapel."

Jay rushed to the back and found the two trunks. Justin helped him pull them off the shelf and when they opened them they found a mass of iron. Chains connected handles to balls with thin openings.

Jamie grabbed a handle and raised it high. "These look more like spokeless maces."

Jay grabbed the ball with both hands and turned, opening the container. "Monks and priests would put sage in here and walk the streets at night. The smoke was believed to send evil spirits running."

"So what are we going to use them for?" Samantha asked.

"We're going to patrol, and these will keep The Devil from getting too close."

"What if it gets too close anyway?" April asked.

"That's what the holy water is for," Jay answered.

Jamie reached down and grabbed a second ward. "Well, if it could get that close then I'm going to rig one to my back."

Justin pointed and waved his finger at Jamie. "That's a great idea. Everyone grab two."

Armed with a ward in each hand, the group went back to the chapel to meet Father O'Brian. He was waiting for them by the altar with several green bottles, enough for each one of the crew to have at least two.

"I would suggest heading to The Candle Shop for the sage. Maria usually keeps a large stock of it there."

Before Jay could say thanks, their phones started to buzz and ding from notifications. Father O'Brian looked on as they thumbed through their notifications.

"I may not be an expert on phones, but I know something must be going on when everyone in a group gets notified like that. What's happening?" Father O'Brian asked.

Jay held up his phone. "Door cameras all over town caught this person walking around town."

Jay revealed an image of a man with a baggy, lightly-colored shirt, raggedy pants that stopped at the knees, and no shoes. If those details weren't enough to set the mystery man apart from anyone else in town, his head movement was. The man had his head tilted to the sky and was moving quickly from right to left.

"I think we found The Jersey Devil," Jay informed.

Father O'Brian nodded. "It appears so. His dress is rather usual." He pointed at the screen. "Even a transient would be wearing more, especially at night during this time of the year."

"Thanks for all the help Father O' Brian, but we must be off," Jay said.

"Stay together and stay safe."

Jay and his friends left the church, visited the Candle Shop, and bought enough sage to last them a month. Since The Devil hunted under the cover of darkness, they were forced to wait for dusk to conduct a hunt of their own.

Jay looked at the time on his phone and glanced over at the window. He grabbed his bag and said, "Let's get going."

"So, is there anything that resembles a game plan?" Justin asked.

Jay pulled out a lighter, lit the sage, and placed it in the spirit wards. "In ten minutes one of you will light yours and then another in ten more minutes. This will help ensure that a continual fog floats around us."

"Good plan, but who's the next target?" Samantha asked.

"I don't know." Jay proceeded to walk down his sidewalk. "In all of my research, I never found a pattern of victims. It was always the sins but never in a real order."

"Well, let's think of people who fit the bill," April suggested.

"Wrath and lust could be any one of the athletes," Justin noted.

"To be fair, wrath could go for anyone who Terrance and his minions picked on or bullied throughout the years," Jamie corrected.

Samantha raised her hand. "If we see The Devil with Terrance, do we really need to stop him?" Everyone stopped moving except Samantha. When she finally realized she was alone on this thought, she turned and asked, "What? I mean, come on. Who wasn't thinking it?"

Jamie shrugged. "I was, and it's been on my mind a lot. Honestly, I wish he and his minions were the only ones taken."

"Look, I get it. They've been horrible to all of us but we still have to try—"

The buzzing and dings of phones interrupted Jay, and once more they looked on to the news that someone had been taken.

"How could someone be taken this quickly?" April looked at the sky and then at her phone. "The sun set like five minutes ago. He would have been seen walking anywhere around town."

"Guys, it was Justice. She's the last house on her road," Jay said.

"And there's a small patch of woods butting up to her backyard. It's perfect for hiding and striking at the right moment," Jamie added.

April threw her hands up in a huff. "So what now?"

Jay scratched his head and asked, "What was Justice on the list of sins?"

Without hesitation, Samantha answered, "Pride."

"Really? She—" Jay was interrupted again by notifications. Everyone except Jamie looked at their phones.

"How is this possible?" Samantha asked.

"I don't know. This doesn't make sense," Jay said.

"What?" Everyone turned to Jamie, who shrugged his shoulders in response.

"They're saying The Devil took another one tonight," Jay explained.

"So, who was it?" Jamie asked.

Looking up from her phone, the bright white light illuminated April's face. She answered, "Seth."

"But which one is Seth? And why two? Has he ever taken two in one night like this?" Samantha turned to Jay, clearly wanting answers.

"I don't know. I mean, he could be wrath, lust, or greed. Gluttony and Sloth don't apply to him." Jay started scratching his head. "He's never taken two. Always one at a time. Seven sins, seven days, and seven victims. That's the pattern. Every time." Jay paused. "No, that's not true. He took Amber and Tiffany on one night and Jeremy and Nichole on another, but other than that he followed the pattern."

Justin threw up his hands. "So why now? What makes this and the last time so different?"

"I don't know. It doesn't make sense."

Jamie held up his hand. "Guys, I think I may know. I mean, maybe. It's just a thought."

"Then spill it," April shouted.

"So, The Devil takes a victim and sucks their essence out of them, right? So, it's not far-fetched to think he consumes all they know."

"Anyone else not following?" Justin looked around.

"If The Devil knows what everyone he consumes does, then he's not just a possessed guy from four hundred years ago. He's seen all the technology updates and knows people have seen him.

He knows we're looking for him and he knows who to hunt," Jamie explained.

"I missed it. I can't believe I missed it." Jay tugged at his hair, bent to the ground, and began jumping up and down. "I can't believe I missed it."

"Calm down." April placed her hand on Jay's shoulder. "People already think you're the new Crazy Carl. You jumping up and down while grabbing your hair adds to the argument."

"You guys don't get it. I assumed he was bound to a pattern or process like a code, but it was just a coincidence based on the times. He followed it because he never had to deviate from it. There weren't home security cameras of any kind, cell phones, or social media that spread alerts in seconds like there are today."

"So, what do we do?" Justin asked.

"We can't keep wandering about the streets with the hope that we'll see him," Samantha said.

"Yeah, I mean what will we do even if we find him?" April held up her spirit ward. "These are used to keep it away, so what are we doing?"

Jay shrugged his shoulders. "I guess I just wanted to make sure he didn't take any of us. I need you guys." April cleared her throat. "And girls. You're my family."

"I don't want to break up the heartfelt moment but I have an idea." All heads turned to Jamie. "Use me as bait."

"You can't be serious. There's no way you're on his list." April looked around but no one agreed with her.

"Ya'll know I love being me and I wouldn't change a thing, but to The Devil, I'm gluttony." Jamie looked around. "I've got to do this."

Samantha was shaking her head, almost violently. "No, we can't." Samantha's head stopped shaking and was followed by a hard stare. "What's wrong with you all? What if we can't stop The Devil? What if Jamie gets absorbed into it?"

"What if we stop him?" Jay asked. "What if this is the best shot—the only shot—we have? Where will we be in thirty years? No one has bothered to stop The Devil while hundreds of kids have disappeared."

"Ugh, he's right," Justin muttered. "If we don't try something, then no one will. It will just become another copycat serial kidnapper. We know the truth, and we know it'll come for the next generation."

"I don't like it," Samantha reiterated.

"Sam," April softly said. "They're right. If we don't stop him now, then our kids could be next."

Jamie walked over and grabbed Samantha by the shoulders. "In the end, it doesn't matter what happens to me. What matters is that we tried."

Samantha wrapped her arms around Jamie. "Fine, but I still don't like it."

9

The Jersey Devil: Part VI

October 27th, 2023

Jay pounded on his sister's door and yelled, "Wakey, wakey!"
Samantha jerked open the door and shouted, "What?"
"Breakfast, then the War Room."
The door slammed in Jay's face. He shrugged his shoulders and went to start cooking, if one could call it that. This morning's breakfast involved toasting waffles, microwaving bacon, and opening pre-packaged muffins. After the feast, they followed Jay to the war room. A table had been placed in the middle of the room and had a host of objects resting on a map.

"How do you find time for all of this?" Jamie asked.

"I hate to say it this way but with two people taken in the same night, I felt safe The Devil wouldn't take a third, so I came down here after ya'll fell asleep."

"What are you going to do with yourself after we banish The Devil?" April asked.

Jay waved his finger at April. "I've wondered that myself, but we need to focus." Everyone joined Jay around the table. "This is night number three and I don't think he's going to take someone."

"Why not?" Samantha asked.

"I think the alert level will be too high. Last night he caught all of us by surprise but everyone will be on high alert."

April's phone dinged. She looked at the message and held it up. "Not everyone. Terrance is throwing a party in Seth's honor."

"So, is the taking of someone back on the table?" Justin asked.

"I think it's safe to say it is," Jay answered.

"There's no way we can stop the party, so we need to make me more appealing than those at the party."

"There's not enough time for that." Jay pointed to the items on the table. "We need salt, paint, and holy water."

"What's the Hot Wheels for?" Justin asked.

"They represent the pesticide misters." Jay moved the two Hot Wheel cars to opposite sides of the map. "As you all know, Cork was initially laid out to symbolize a cross surrounded by a circle." Jay drew his fingers around the map. "We will fill the misters with holy water and they will drive around town in opposite directions."

"The mist will create a barrier that will trap The Devil within the town," April explained.

Jay pointed to his nose. "They will continue to circle the town and Jamie will be here in the center." Jay moved a green Sorry game piece to the center of the map. "The rest of us will be here."

Jay picked up blue game pieces and explained, "Justin will be on Main Street to the north and April to the south. Samantha will be on Founders Street from the west and I'll come from the east. Once The Devil passes, we'll light our spirit wards and head to Jamie."

"I get that the holy mist and wards will keep The Devil from moving forward, but what's protecting me from getting eaten?"

Justin placed a hand on Jamie's shoulder. "Don't look at it like you're going to get eaten. It's more like *Hocus Pocus* than *Dawn on the Dead.*"

Jamie shook his head. "That's not comforting."

"Jamie won't get *Hocus Pocus*— Pocused— Pocust—" April threw up her hands with frustration. "He won't get the *Hocus Pocus* treatment because we're going to stop The Devil before he gets close to Jamie, right Jay?"

"I mean, yeah, but he's going to get close to Jamie."

April's voice quivered as she asked, "How close?"

Jay dismissed the question and pointed to an image on the table. "From my research, I found a variety of symbols that ward off evil or trap it."

"Like the same symbol does both?" April asked.

Jay nodded. "This here is a hexafoil and evil cannot cross it. However, if the hexafoil is drawn around the evil then it cannot escape its boundaries." Jay pointed to the center. "Once we have the supplies we need, we will paint this symbol but leave a gap on my side of Founders Street."

"Why a gap?" Justin asked.

April smacked Justin on the arm. "Keep up, will you? The

Devil can't enter if the symbol is closed. Once it's inside, Jay will close the symbol and The Devil will be trapped."

"Then what?" Justin asked.

"I found a chant that should separate the demon from the man, but I don't know what happens after that?"

Justin's eyes widened in fear. "Could the demon jump into us?"

Jay shrugged his shoulders. "I don't know. Anything documented is more like folklore than fact, so it's hard to say what will work."

"So, how are we getting all this done?" Samantha asked.

Jay told them his plan and the crew spent the rest of the day going from house to house asking for salt and white paint. He explained that the two will combine to not only paint the hexafoil but the salt will add an extra layer of protection. They met back in Jay's War Room with the results of their efforts. Jamie and April were the last to arrive.

"We got two gallons of paint but no one was willing to give up any salt," Jamie informed.

"That brings up to six gallons of paint and just over a hundred pounds of salt."

"How did ya'll get over a hundred pounds?" Jamie stretched.

"Not us." Samantha pointed to Jay. "He got two fifty-pound bags."

"From?" Jamie asked.

"Uncle Nick's Diner. He was a big fan of Carl's, and now of mine, so he was more than happy to donate." Jay turned to Justin. "Any luck convincing your uncle to let us use the misters?"

"None. He said they're too valuable to let us play with for a couple of hours," Justin answered.

"So, what now? We can't just go paint the center of main street, and I'm not going to that party."

"Sam's right. There's too much to risk in both. The sheriff will make us stop painting and something's going to happen at the party," April cautioned.

"I know, and as much as I hate to say this, we need to wait until Jamie is the last one to be taken, but—"

"Come on man, no buts. Buts are always bad," Justin interrupted.

"But," Jay continued. "We need to sleep in the same room from now on. We'll bunk in the living room and put salt around the doors and windows."

Everyone agreed, and they prepared for the night. They ate, laughed till they cried, and prepped the house for sunset. All was quiet until April got a "going live" notification from Jasmine.

"Guys, Jasmine is going live from the party," April announced.

Jay quickly found the feed and cast it on the TV. The scene was chaotic. Lights rapidly flashed while multicolored party lights haphazardly sprayed their rays all over the room. Though the camera was pointed away from Jasmine, it was clear that she was crouching on the floor, and the camera shook, signaling that she was scared out of her mind. The music was loud but not loud enough to drown out the screams, crying, and beating of fists on what one could assume were locked doors.

Though the lights made it difficult to see, The Devil was approaching. There was no mistaking the red eyes of evil, and despite its enormous size, several tried to attack it. Shovels and 2x4s crashed against its armor-like skin and they snapped upon contact. Suddenly, The Devil disappeared. Jasmine started to stand when bodies came crashing to the ground. Her scream was deafening and she immediately dropped back to the floor. The Devil dove to the ground, but it wasn't alone. One could see it was carrying three bodies, and before anything else could happen, the feed went black.

"He took three." Justin's voice was grim.

"Who were they?" Samantha asked.

Jay looked at the comments that were pouring in. Someone said it had Terrance and another said one looked like Tiffany. No one said anything about the third. Jay clicked watch again and fast-forwarded it to the end. He paused it on The Devil and its victims. Everyone leaned forward to examine the victims.

"Terrance," Jamie whispered.

"Tiffany," April gasped.

"Oh man," Jamie whined. "It's Samuel."

"Wrath, lust, and sloth," Jay said.

"I thought I would be okay with The Devil taking Terrance, but look at his face," Samantha said. "That's a type of fear that I don't wish on anyone."

"Yeah, I don't feel good about this," Justin added.

Justin's phone rang. "Hey...yeah, I saw it...Yeah, you sure?... I'll let you know." Justin hung up the phone. "My uncle saw the live stream. He and my cousin will drive the misters. We just need to fill them in on the plan."

"Good, and I know it's going to be tough, but let's get some sleep," Jay suggested.

He turned off the TV and lights, but no one went right to

sleep. The glow of their phones shone brightly into the early hours.

October 31, 2023

Three days passed and the trap had been set. Jay and his crew painted the hexafoil on the road and left a small gap for Jay to close it. Justin's uncle and cousin took their positions at the edge of town, and Jamie took his position in the center of the hexafoil. The others took their mark on their respective streets.

The sunlight faded, signaling that it was time, and the town was all but abandoned.

April waited in the entranceway of the pharmacy. The overhang blocked out any moonlight, essentially making her invisible. It was just a few moments after the sun fell that she heard the heavy steps of The Devil. She watched as the man-beast passed, and it was as Carl had said... The Devil was the size of a giant and it had horns like those of a ram.

She waited until he was well past the building when she texted everyone: "He's coming to you, Jamie."

Seconds later she got a reply. "Light the wards."

April pulled out her lighter and lit the sage in both wards. She cautiously advanced behind The Devil. April noticed The Devil's advance was quickening. She dropped a ward and called Jay.

"What's wrong?" Jay asked.

"He moving faster," she warned.

"Call the others. I've got to get into position."

April started running after The Devil, and before she could

call Samantha, The Devil arrived at the hexafoil. Step by step she saw it getting closer to Jamie as he sat vulnerable and cross-legged on the ground. He aimed his flashlight at the sky, which acted like the bat signal for demons.

April looked at Jay. With brush in hand, he closed the hexafoil. Slowly, she began moving toward Samantha.

The Devil reached out to Jamie, but its hand stopped. He pulled its arm back and launched it forward. Again, its hand failed to reach its target.

Over and over the Devil tried to get its prey, but repeatedly failed. Jamie pointed to the ground and the ring of salt that surrounded him—a fail-safe to ensure he wasn't taken.

Jay yelled, "In five." April opened the voice memo on her phone. "Four." She pressed the volume up on her phone. "Three." She finally met Samantha. "Two." They took a step into the hexafoil. "One." They advanced toward The Devil. "Play."

They all hit play.

Their phones echoed a recording of Father O'Brian reading from an exorcism text. April didn't know what was being said but she knew it was hurting the demon. It began growling, yelling, screeching, and covering its ears.

April and Samantha were less than five feet away when The Devil turned to run away. He ran to the edge of the hexafoil and immediately fell to the ground as if it hit a brick wall. The hexafoil worked. It kept The Devil from fleeing.

With spirit wards in hand, they surrounded the demon.

Though it appeared to be in pain, April thought the exorcism text wasn't working. It wasn't until she focused on its hands that she realized she was wrong. Its black skin was peeling back to reveal Caucasian flesh underneath. With each word spoken, more was unveiled, until a beam of white light shot in the air.

April covered her eyes. When she removed her hand, there were two beings in front of her. Both were the size of an average adult. The all-black being cowered to the ground. Everyone could tell it was afraid. The other was John, and he was the opposite. He smiled and looked as though he had the weight of the world taken off his shoulders.

The ground started to shake beneath the black mass. The shaking gave way to cracks and through the cracks came a hand. It latched on to its throat and pulled it through the hole.

"Thank you," John said. Everyone stopped the recording. "I've wanted that for so long. I owe you a debt that I'm afraid I won't be able to repay."

"If it makes you feel better, we didn't do it for you. We did it for our kids and those who come after them," Samantha explained.

John nodded. "I understand, but I'm appreciative nonetheless."

"What happened to you?" Jay asked.

"I swear to you and all that is holy that I never harmed a soul before my death. I was angry and wanted revenge. Once the world started to turn black, I was approached by this demon and it made me a deal to get my revenge." John took a deep breath. "At first, it felt so good to watch them suffer as I did, but the pleasure quickly faded with time. I was taking the lives of those who had no connection to what happened to me, but I wasn't allowed to stop. It owned me."

"It would be easy to be mad at you, but we understand," Jay said.

"You do?" John questioned.

"Yeah, I mean, we don't like what happened, but we don't know how it feels to be you. You experienced a betrayal that none of us have, so who knows how we would've reacted if it happened to one of us," Jay explained.

"Yes, well, thank you for understanding." John looked around and asked, "What happens now?"

Jay shrugged his shoulders. "You cross over I suppose."

"I have a lot to be judged for."

April cleared her throat. "I don't know what awaits us, but if we are to be judged, then I'd like to think you'd be judged on your life before and not what it became."

John smiled and began to fade away.

"Can anyone else believe that we just stopped The Jersey Devil?" Justin asked.

"I can," Jay answered.

"Well, we know where John is off to, but what's next for us?" Jamie asked.

"I wasn't going to say anything yet, but I've done some research on a rural town in Pennsylvania that is claiming to have multiple Bigfoot sightings."

Other Works by D. W. Saur

Dark Days

It has been centuries since The Great War and the four sects of Sori have come to live in relative peace and harmony. Sori's Caomhnóir judges the occasional crimes in Bala's markets and the severity of punishments deter the majority from temptation. Besides the crimes committed in Cala's boundaries, the sects of Sori saw an era of prosperity.

Though the sects prospered, this euphoric state was not destined to last forever. A dark, almost ghost-like, figure arrives in Sori and begins to upset the balance the land has come to enjoy. The figure plots and manipulates members of the Galenvarg and Veirlintu sects into rebellion. Upon the arrival of the figure, the Goddess Nantosuelta selects a Leigheasan named Maya as her chosen one to eliminate the threat and prevent another Great War.

To many Leigheasan, Maya was not capable of being a chosen one. She had not completed their rite of passage, was powerless, and isolated herself from those her age. With Nantosuelta's blessing, Maya begins her quest to find her powers, prevent war, and establish herself as a leader among the Leigheasan.

Accolades for Dark Days

2022 Book Excellence Awards: Finalist in Young Adult Fiction

2021 Readers' Favorite Book Awards: Honorable Mention in the Young Adult category for Action

2021 American Fiction Awards: Finalist in the Epic/High category

2021 Feathered Quill Book Awards: Finalist in the category of Science Fiction/Fantasy

2021 Feathered Quill Book Awards: Finalist in the category of Teens (13-18)

2020 Royal Dragonfly Book Award: Dark Days won a Royal DragonFly award in the category of Young Adult Fiction

2020 Royal Dragonfly Book Award: Dark Days won a Royal DragonFly award in the category of Science Fiction/Fantasy
5 Star Reader's Favorite Book Seal
4 Star Literary Titan Book Seal

Reviews for Dark Days

Literary Titan: "Dark Days plunges readers into the depths of a complex dark fantasy world that begs to be explored. D.W. Saur sets up intriguing characters that face some enormous challenges, but watching them overcome them is half the fun of this adventure novel."

Kirkus Review: "An impressive first installment with a remarkable, series-worthy hero."

BookLife: "Like The Hunger Games and Earth's Children, Dark Days follows the adventures of a young heroine armed with intelligence, pluck, and extraordinary talents. YA readers will recognize Maya as an exemplar of Girl Power Lit."

Book Excellence Awards: "Readers will fall in love with and root for Maya, who is a powerful and magnetic character. They will also revel in the wit and humor in the story along with action and adventure sequences, shown by the clever dialogue and fight scenes."

Metal Like Me

As a child, Vinny was unaware of his and his family's difference but, as he got older, Vinny noticed that he was, in fact, not like other children. Because he was a metalhead, Vinny had a hard time making friends in elementary school. This changed as he entered middle school, where Vinny finally found friends who were metal like him. The group did not have an easy time as they were bullied or picked on for much of their first year. Tired of being viewed as different, Vinny came up with a plan to show their classmates that he and his friends weren't that different. Join Vinny as he shares his story of bullying, difference, coping, and perseverance.

Accolades for Metal Like Me

2020 Purple Dragonfly: Honorable Mention
2020 Story Monsters Approved: School Life
5 Star Reader's Favorite Book Seal
5 Star Literary Titan Book Seal

Reviews for Metal Like Me

Readers' Favorite 5-star Review by Mamta Madhavan: "Metal Like Me by D.W. Saur is an adorable story about being different, bullying, coping with differences, self-acceptance, strength, courage, and perseverance. Danielle Green's illustrations are as charming as the plot and breathe life into the story and characters. This book will encourage children who are facing difficulties at school because of being different to become strong and tackle their problems wisely. The message in the book is good and the author's approach to it is refreshing and original. Vinny's character portrayal is real, relatable, and strong. Tutors and parents can use the story to help children accept their differences and get past the struggles of their initial years in a good way."

Literary Titan 5-star Review: "*Metal Like Me* by D. W. Saur is a sweet story about acceptance. The author has lovingly crafted an endearing story that will inspire children to learn about diversity and inclusion. Kids will learn that being unique is a gift and we must all embrace it." "*Metal Like Me* approaches the topic of bullying in a unique way that makes it easy for parents and children to start a discussion. I definitely recommend this well-written, short, and easy-to-understand book as it will teach children a positive way to identify themselves. The illustrations by Danielle Green are beautifully simple with a rough sketch-like illustration that will make it easy for kids to relate to. The fantastic artwork excellently captures the unique voice in this charismatic children's story."

Amazon Reviewer: "Put it on every middle school bookshelf – Loved this book! There are so many lessons here for all middle school kiddos and those around that age. A great conversation starter!"

The Untold: Stories from World War II

What if the villain isn't who you think he was? What if you are called to risk it all by going behind enemy lines? What if your skills require you to take another's life? The Untold: Stories from World War II is a historical fiction novella divided into three stories that address these questions with a series of twists.

In A Crime Against Humanity, a courtroom full of press and attendees glare at the man accused of murdering thousands of Jews at the concentration camp known as Schwarzes Wasser. Commandant Karl Müller admits to every horrible deed committed in enough detail that his fate is sealed. However, there's more to Karl's story than just the crimes committed.

When Karl's story ends, veteran Luke Taylor retells his story in Flashbacks. Born into a military family, Luke, along with almost fifty other boys, was groomed to be spies in the mission codenamed Project Loki. It took decades for Luke to realize that infiltrating the Nazi war machine was the easiest part of his mission.

The Untold comes full circle in The Eastern Front when a graduate student unlocks the story between the cryptic pages of Oksana Gribanov's diary. The diary reveals her time of service as a sharpshooter during the siege in Leningrad and beyond.

Reviews for The Untold

Amazon Reviewer: "Saur upped his game with The Untold and is proving a master at novellas. These three stories are short, powerful, and could have could have been a full novel in their own right. Though you're wanting more, each story captivates you from the start. Personally, I thought A Crime Against Humanity was the best. I don't want to spoil anything but I was shocked at serval points in the story and the way he pulled it together was nothing short of brilliant."

Amazon Reviewer: "I was asked by this author to read the ARC for this book. When I reviewed the title and the contents, I actually told him that I may not be the best suited to give a fair and honest review. I have a personal issue reading anything war-related and I really wanted him to get the best outcome possible for his book. He asked me to read it anyway as he really wanted to appeal to a wider audience and he felt that he had done so in this writing. Wow.... Along with five stars, I cannot explain how good this book was. It was very well done, historically accurate, and definitely will reach a wide span audience! It was a little emotional at times for me but I just didn't want to put the book down."

Amazon Reviewer: "D.W Saur delivers another fantastic read. Taking you on a journey through WWII with fantastic story-telling and characters. It's hard to put down once you start."

Just Friends

The Fantastic Four leaped out of the pages of the comics and straight into suburbia. Justin, Jill, Sam, and Amanda were born in the same year, lived on the same street, and were insepaɹable during their early childhood. Their bond became tested in middle school when Amanda started to drift from the group. By the time they entered high school, Amanda was rarely seen with her childhood friends.

Throughout high school, Sam was officially placed in Amanda's friend zone and only spoke to him when she needed a shoulder to cry on. No matter how badly he was treated Sam clung to the hope of a relationship but that all changed after being stood up as her date for senior prom.

Sam was finally tired of just being Amanda's friend so he severed ties and moved on to college. There he meets Jennifer and the two begin making the type of memories Sam once wished he could have shared with Amanda. During Sam's freshman year, Amanda kept her distance and they went over a year without communication of any kind. No DMs, no texts, and no calls were made by either of them.

This all ends when Amanda comes knocking on Sam's dorm expecting to have his comforting ear once more. However, Amanda discovers Sam has more than just a girlfriend. Sam has been holding on to a secret that will forever change their friendship.

Reviews for Just Friends

Amazon Reviewer: "My favorite quote in the book is, "Music, regardless of the genre, was the one thing that embraced the individual instead of using or criticizing them." I absolutely loved how the story was wrapped up in the music; it was as if music itself was an additional character. The story also ends with a recorded jam session -- a memory and legacy that will last forever for those involved. The story itself was very touching, and the character arcs were all very believable. I would love to have Sam as a friend!"

Amazon Reviewer: "This book was very hard to put down. DW Sauer had me traveling back to my past experiences with friends growing up, and also nostalgia for my life in Virginia! The friendships captured in this book are genuine. Thank you

DW Sauer for a great ride and I look forward to your further works."

Amazon Reviewer: "I loved this book! D.W. Saur Just doesn't disappoint with his beautiful stories... This story is beautifully written and will be difficult to put down. A tearjerker with a range of emotions. Highly recommended read."

The Last Christmas

Sara's marriage was on the rocks for years. After a long shift, she arrived home to a note saying, "Locks have been changed. Your stuff is on the porch."

Sara grabbed her bags, got back in the car, and headed aimlessly up the highway. For Sale signs act like a homing beacon and lead Sara to a rundown Christmas tree farm. A vision of a farm that brought Santa's village to reality ensued. The owner of the land agrees to sell a portion of the farm for Sara's promise to revive it to its former glory.

With the Herculean task of running and renovating, help unexpectedly comes when a former childhood visitor of the farm named Jack arrives. The duo is committed to bringing a North

Pole experience to all but amidst a budding relationship in turbulent times.

Reviews for The Last Christmas

Amazon Reviewer: "During the holidays, I love to indulge in a book or two with all the Christmas feels. This year I chose The Last Christmas and it turned out to be the heartwarming experience I was looking for. It was like comfort food for the brain. After Sarah's marriage falls apart, she starts her life anew by trying to bring a rundown tree farm back to life by transforming it into Santa's Village. But as obstacles continue to get thrown in her way, she must lean on her friends and community for support if her dream ever stands a chance of succeeding. This story was a pleasant combination of romance, tradition, heart, and perseverance, leaving me feeling uplifted and hopeful. If you enjoy Hallmark movies and stories like We Bought A Zoo, then you'll love this book! The story had steady pacing, loveable characters, and a refreshing outlook, not on the selfish ambition for success, but the passion to achieve a dream and be able to give back to the community. That life is bigger than just ourselves, and that we can all work together to be happy and fulfilled. I recommend this book to anyone who loves books full of holiday magic!"

Amazon Reviewer: "This was a fast and easy read and one you'll devour in just a couple sittings if not one. D.W. Sauer does an impressive job of teaching us that when we hit rock bottom, there really is nowhere else to go but up, but in order to turn our life around, we must put pride aside and work hard to achieve the desired goal. I loved this story about friendship, family, and family traditions. Growing up, my family had, and still has, their own Christmas traditions, so I could relate to the main character's desire to grow a family Christmas tree farm into something truly magical. The only thing that would have made this read even better, is if I had read it during the Christmas season, but that just means I might have to plan another reread at the end of 2020 to fully appreciate the seasonal aspects of this wonderful and lovable story."

Return To Christmas Town

Available December 2023

Though the founders of Christmas Town are gone, the spirit of the North Pole experience lives on through their family. T.J., Sara's oldest grandchild, took on a larger role as the third major owner of Christmas Town. He picked up where his grandmother left off in continuing the traditions of the business and serving the community. Christmas Town expanded and was thriving but little did T.J. and his family know that it was the calm before the storm.

Sydney Garcia of Garcia Entertainment shocked the residents of Fenton with the company's plans to build a resort and amusement park next to Christmas Town. The plans included all that Christmas Town has to offer, but bigger and better. For some, this means jobs and a way to provide for their family but for others, it means competition that could run them out of business.

Sydney faces off with T.J. as both try to keep their dream alive, but the road takes an unexpected turn.

What's New and Where to Follow

Instagram
@d.w.saur
@polarpressbooks
X (Twitter)
@dw_saur
@polarpressbooks
YouTube
@PolarPressPresents
Goodreads
@dwsaur
Website
https://dwsaur.com/
https://polarpressbooks.com/

www.ingramcontent.com/pod-product-compliance
Lightning Source LLC
Chambersburg PA
CBHW071435300726
48976CB00004B/1337